Pammie Pigeon

David M. Sargent, Jr., and his friends live in Northwest Arkansas. His writing career began in 1995 with a cruel joke being played on his mother. The friends pictured with him are (from left to right) Vera, Buffy, and Mary.

Dave Sargent is a lifelong resident of the small town of Prairie Grove, Arkansas. A fourth-generation dairy farmer, Dave began writing in early December 1990. He enjoys the outdoors and has a real love for birds and animals.

Pammie Pigeon

By

Dave Sargent
and
David M. Sargent, Jr.

Beyond The End
By
Sue Rogers

Illustrated by
Jane Lenoir

Ozark Publishing, Inc.
P.O. Box 228
Prairie Grove, AR 72753

Cataloging-in-publication data

Sargent, Dave, 1941-
  Pammie Pigeon / by Dave Sargent ; illustrated by
Jane Lenoir. – Prairie Grove, AR : Ozark Publishing,
c2003.
    vi, 42 p. : col. ill. ; 21 cm.   (Feather tale series)

  "Keep your cool"—Cover.
  SUMMARY: Pammie Pigeon has a quiet day in the
country until she is shocked to learn that Peggy
Porcupine has been chewing the bark off Farmer
John's favorite trees. Includes factual information
about pigeons.
    ISBN: 1-56763-741-8 (hc)
           1-56763-742-6 (pbk)
    RL 2.4 ; IL 2-8

  [1. Pigeons—Fiction. 2. Porcupines—Fiction.] I.
Lenoir, Jane, 1950- ill. II. Title. III. Series.

  PZ10.3.S243Paj 2003
  [Fic]—dc21   99-089897

Inspired by

pigeons, who strut around, acting so proud.

Dedicated to

students who have walked through a park and watched pigeons prancing around. It's fun to listen to them, too. I hope you, like pigeons, can always be proud of your actions.

Foreword

When Pammie Pigeon yearns for a few quiet days in the country, she meets ole Barney the Bear Killer and Peggy Porcupine. Pammie is shocked to learn that the cute little porcupine has been chewing the bark off Farmer John's favorite trees!

Contents

If you would like to have an author of The Feather Tale Series visit your school, free of charge, call 1-800-321-5671 or 1-800-960-3876.

One

Pammie Meets Peggy

As the sun crept slowly upward, long lines of cars impatiently waited at a signal light. It should turn green! Minutes passed before the motorists realized the light was stuck on red. Suddenly, angry voices, car horns, and a police siren exploded through the calm. Soon a policeman was directing traffic through the problem area, but the progress was very slow. From her temporary perch on the top of a tall building, Pammie Pigeon looked down and groaned.

"I must need a vacation from the hustle and bustle of this big ole city," she muttered. "Usually, the confusion and chaos don't bother me."

Seconds later, Pammie Pigeon was airborne. "I'm out of here," she thought. "A nice peaceful day in the country will cure what ails me."

Minutes later, she was soaring high above the city. She flew westerly toward the woodlands. While gliding over a peaceful farm, she decided to land in the yard of the farmhouse. She landed in a tree and settled on a branch near the trunk.

"Aw," she murmured. "A day of sunshine and clean air with relaxed country folk is just what I need. Why, I feel better already!"

Suddenly Pammie was hit by a falling object. It bounced off her back and fell to the ground. She shook her head and ruffled her sleek feathers. "Probably just a small pine cone," she decided. But mere seconds later, another thud shook her body . . . and another . . . and another.

"Pine cones do not fall off the trees in big bunches!" she exclaimed.

As she looked up, a large piece of tree bark hit her between the eyes.

Pammie shouted, "Okay! Who is throwing bark at me, and why?"

"I-I'm so sorry," a high-pitched voice answered. "N-No one was below me when I started to work up here. I d-didn't know you were down there. Honest!"

"I just left a big noisy city," Pammie scolded, "to get away from construction and chaos and such. What in the world are you doing up there anyway?"

Pammie heard a loud rustling sound approaching from overhead. The unfamiliar noise frightened her, and she spread her wings for flight.

"P-p-please don't leave," the voice stuttered. "I-I am afraid to be by myself. You see, that's why I was gnawing at the b-bark. It's b-because gnawing c-calms my nerves."

A furry critter started climbing down the trunk toward Pammie. Sharp barbs were protruding from within its soft brown hair. As the varmint moved, the barbs rubbed together, creating the rustling sound.

"Who are you?" Pammie asked. "On second thought, what are you?"

The furry little critter giggled nervously. "M-my name is Peggy. I'm a p-p-porcupine."

"Well, it's nice to meet you, Peggy Porcupine," Pammie Pigeon said graciously. "Please tell me. Why are you so nervous?"

"Well, it's b-because," the little porcupine cried, "because I just am. M-maybe it's because I just left my m-mama's nest."

Pammie immediately understood, and she carefully patted Peggy on the head with one wing.

"I know that leaving home can be very scary," Pammie said quietly. "But you better learn to relax before you have a nervous breakdown, little girl!"

The youngster's body trembled and shook, and a tear slowly trickled down her cheek.

"I-I just w-want to sh-sh-show my m-mama that I'm a big girl now, and I-I am capable of t-t-taking care of m-myself. B-Besides," the poor little porcupine whined, "sh-she makes me go to bed t-too early!"

Pammie tried to hide a smile. "That is a very serious situation for a youngster of your caliber."

"Y-Y-Yes it is!" Peggy said in a loud voice. "V-V-Very serious!"

"It is important for you to think clearly and remain calm if you are going to live alone in this big world," Pammie explained. "A calm attitude creates a smart sensible mind, but fear and bad nerves are dangerous."

"I-I-I want to be just like you!" Peggy Porcupine stated as she patted one paw nervously on the branch. "J-J-Just like y-you!"

Two

Barney Chases Pammie

Suddenly Pammie heard the front door of the house slam shut. Farmer John and Molly walked across the yard, laughing and talking as they looked at each flower, shrub, and tree. Pammie saw Farmer John suddenly stop and stare at the ground beneath her tree. His frown warned her of his displeasure.

"Molly," Farmer John called, "Look at this. The bark's been eaten off this pine tree, and it'll die if we don't do something."

The woman hurried toward him. "Oh, John," she said quietly, "you are right. There has been a lot of damage done to the prettiest tree in our yard. What animal would do such a thing?"

Farmer John slowly shifted his attention upward. Pammie gulped as his gaze stopped on her.

"Ssshhh," she whispered to the little porcupine. "Be real quiet, and perhaps he won't notice you."

The little porcupine gulped and hiccupped, and her teeth began to chatter. Then her body began to shake and shiver. The clattering chattering noise grew in intensity as Farmer John moved nearer to the tree. All of a sudden the little limb that was holding Peggy collapsed beneath her unsteady weight. The poor little porcupine squealed in terror as she fell through the foliage and landed right on top of Farmer John's hat. The impact knocked him off his feet, and both man and porcupine hit the ground with a thud.

"Ouch!" Farmer John yelled.

"Run, Peggy!" Pammie Pigeon screamed. "Run! Run as if your life depended on it!" In a hoarse whisper, she added, "Because it does!"

She looked down and saw that the only damage was to the man's hat. Farmer John's hat was covered with the porcupine's sharp spines. Her gaze quickly shifted to Peggy. The little thing was running blindly toward Barney the Bear Killer, who was napping near the front gate.

"Not that direction!" Pammie screamed. "Turn, Peggy! Turn!"

Peggy veered off to the left and scurried toward the barn. The tired dog opened one eye before standing up to give chase. Pammie instantly flew into action. She swooped low over the dog's head, and he accepted the challenge.

A moment later, pigeon and dog disappeared into the nearby woods, and Peggy ran into the barn.

Soon Pammie returned without the dog. "My low flight through the woods should keep that dog busy for a little while," she thought. "He thinks I'm still there."

"Where are you, little Peggy?" Pammie called. "Come out, and I will take you home to your mama."

There was no answer. Pammie moved nearer to the barn.

"Peggy," she called quietly. "If you'll come out before that dog gets back, I'll help you get home safely."

Moments passed in silence before she saw two eyes peering at her from beneath a burlap bag near the barn door. But a noise from the farmhouse diverted her attention.

"Now I'm ready," Farmer John said, "to meet that porcupine!"

Pammie saw that he was carrying a shotgun, and her heart raced with fear for her newfound friend. She glanced back toward the sack, but there was no sign of Peggy. The pigeon flew to the nearest tree, hoping Farmer John would not enter the barn. She watched him as he checked the area for signs of the renegade porcupine. Then she felt a rising panic as he entered the barn, mere inches from the burlap bag.

"Just stay calm, little Peggy," the pigeon murmured from her high perch in the tree. "Be very quiet and stay calm."

Three

The Tree-Killing Fungus

Minutes later, Farmer John had finished checking the interior of the barn. And now, as he neared the door, he walked right by the burlap sack without even looking at it. He stepped out into the bright sunlight.

"John!" Molly shouted from the front yard. "Did you find him?"

Pammie watched Farmer John shake his head, and she breathed a big sigh of relief.

"No, I didn't find him," the man replied.

Molly ran across the barnyard toward him. Pammie was surprised to see that she was smiling.

"I am glad you didn't find him!" she said cheerfully as she hugged Farmer John. "That little fellow just saved the life of all of our trees, John. I was looking at the bark, and it is infested with a fungus that would have spread and killed every tree on our farm!"

"You know," Farmer John said quietly, "sometimes I feel like the animals are our best friends. I guess I should thank that little porcupine."

Pammie watched the man and woman walk away and enter the house. Then she realized that Peggy was still hiding somewhere within the barn. She flew to the door and peeked inside.

"Little Peggy," she said in a loud proud voice. "You can come out now. Farmer John is not mad at you anymore."

The burlap bag suddenly moved, and the pigeon jumped backward.

"Are you sure, Pammie?" a muffled voice inquired.

"Honest, Peggy," Pammie responded. "As a matter of fact, he wanted to thank you for saving his trees from a fungus!"

"Wow!" Peggy said as she peered from beneath the sack. "How did I do that?"

"Accidentally," Pammie Pigeon murmured. "Accidentally."

Then the pigeon gasped as the little critter skittered out from under the burlap bag and ran toward her.

"Oh, Peggy!" she said hoarsely, "You are a little porcupine, Peggy! But where are your quills?"

The little porcupine sat down and looked at her poor barbless body. Her eyes grew big, and a great big tear rolled down her cheek.

"Oh dear me! M-my p-proud p-porcupine heritage is all g-gone!" she cried. "I c-can't g-go home now! I am t-too embarrassed!"

"Calm down!" the pigeon said. "Don't forget. Bad nerves were the cause of this trouble. Breathe deep."

Pammie walked into the barn and stared down at the burlap bag.

"I found your quills," she said. "Some are stuck in Farmer John's hat, and the rest are caught in this burlap bag."

"Don't you worry, little friend," Pammie said quietly. "You will have new ones before you know it."

"Really?" Peggy asked.

"Yes, really," Pammie Pigeon confirmed. "All you have to do is stay calm and think clearly. Now let me take you home to your mama."

As the pigeon and porcupine slowly moved through the forest, Pammie felt a strong sense of pride for Peggy. She was no longer stuttering, and her nerves were very calm.

"I'm not even going to complain about going to bed early," the little porcupine promised.

After delivering the youngster to a grateful mama, Pammie Pigeon soared upward, slowly winging her way toward the city. "My day in the country may not have been calm," she thought, "but it was one filled with lessons on composure and calm thinking." She landed gracefully on the balcony of a tall building.

"I wonder how little Peggy is tonight," she murmured. "I wonder when she will grow new quills. And I truly wonder if she will remain calm during her next crisis."

Pammie cocked her head to one side and smiled. "Yes, I do believe that she will!"

Hmmm . . .

Four

Pigeon Facts

Pigeons live, for the most part, in warm regions. They are members of a family of birds. There is a smaller species of birds known as doves, but the sizes of pigeons and doves will sometimes overlap.

Pigeons have small heads with short necks. They have stout bodies with short legs, and their plumage is sleek and shiny. They have a fleshy or waxy protuberance, called a cere, at the base of their bills Some live on the ground and some, like Pammie, live in trees. They eat fruit, seeds, acorns and other nuts, and insects. They fly very fast and are known for their cooing call. They build loose nests of twigs, bark, straw, and even weeds; the female lays one or two eggs that are either tan or white.

The best-known species is the common pigeon. Its wild ancestor, native to Asia and Europe, is called the rock dove. It is about 13 inches long, bluish gray above, with black markings on the wings, and its rump is a whitish color. It has a purple breast and is blue on the abdomen. The sides of the neck, especially in males, are iridescent. There are more than 200 domestic breeds that come from this species.

Homing pigeons, which can be very different in color, are bred for their skills at navigating. Among the other domestic breeds is the carrier pigeon. It is sometimes wrongly called the homing pigeon. It is tall and erect, with wattles around the eyes and base of the bill. The frill pigeon is characterized by forward curvature of the tips of the feathers of the neck and body that look a little like ruffles. The pouter can dilate the crop region into a swollen globe. The jacobin, a favorite pet of Queen Victoria, has long neck feathers that form a hood over the head.

The white-crowned pigeon has a white crown on its head. This Caribbean species extends north to southern Florida, the only wild member of its genus found in the eastern United States. The band-tailed pigeon is bigger, almost 15 inches long, and has a range extending from coastal British Columbia and the Rocky Mountains south to Argentina. The passenger pigeon, once very common all across the United States, has been extinct since 1914.

Pigeons that are well known outside the Americas include the crowned pigeons, found in New Guinea and nearby islands. They have an erect crest of modified feathers. The Australian bronze-wings have bronze spots on the wings. The Nicobar pigeons, of islands in the East Indies, have long iridescent dark green hackle feathers on the neck. These hang down over the back and shoulders. Fruit-eating imperial pigeons get up to 20 inches long. There are about 37 species in Asia and the Pacific islands. They vary from multicolored to pure white.

Among the pigeons that are called doves, many can be found in Eurasia and Africa. An Asian species, called the spotted dove, has been very successfully introduced in many parts of the world, including southern California and Hawaii here in North America.

The ringed turtledove is a tame form of uncertain wild origin. The ringed turtledove is found in Florida and California. It is usually buffy with a black ring on the hind neck. A pure white variety has been used in movie scenes of large weddings.

In North America, the most common dove, the mourning dove, is named for its mournful call. It is about 12 inches long, with a brown body, bluish gray wings, and a long, white-tipped tail. It was once found mostly in the open countryside, but it has now become a very familiar sight in urban residential areas.

The little sparrow-sized ground doves are the smallest of all doves. They live in the southern United States and the New World tropics.

GROUND DOVE   INCA DOVE

Scientific classification: Pigeons make up the *Columbidae* family of the order *Columbiformes*. The common pigeon is classified as *Columba livia*, the white-crowned pigeon as *Columba leucocephala*, and the band-tailed pigeon as *Columba fasciata*. The passenger pigeon is classified as *Ectopistes migratorius*. Crowned pigeons make up the genus *Goura*; Australian bronze-wings, the genus *Phaps*; and imperial pigeons, the genus *Ducula*. The Nicobar pigeon is classified as *Caloenas nicobarica*, the spotted dove as *Streptopelia chinensis*, the ringed turtledove as *Streptopelia risoria*, and the mourning dove as *Zenaida macroura*. Ground doves make up the genus *Columbina*.

BEYOND "THE END" . . .

LANGUAGE LINKS

Pammie Pigeon and Peggy Porcupine showed very good manners when they first met and introduced themselves. The way you act around others, using self-control and kindness, is an important part of life. Treat others the way you want to be treated, and you will be a respected and successful person.

Following Pammie and Peggy's example for introducing yourself, make a list of things you could say to greet and introduce yourself to Chipper Jones if he walked into your classroom.

Remember to tell him your name; ask him a question to put him at ease—like "How did you get interested in baseball?" Offer him a seat or offer to take his coat, and compliment him on something he does well in baseball. Be sure to introduce him to your teacher!

Practice with a classmate.

CURRICULUM CONNECTIONS

Your mama sang "Rock-A-Bye, Baby" when she was singing to you. Mama Pigeon has another name for her baby. What is it?

Do you wonder what kind of fungus had infected the tree in Farmer John's yard? Another tree you might be interested in, a Christmas tree, can have problems with fungus and other infestations. Read about farms that grow Christmas trees—over 30 million harvested each year. Find out why one of our favorites, the Scotch pine, suffers many disease problems. See "Pocket Guide to Christmas Tree Diseases" at <www.ncrs.fs.fed.us/epubs/pgctree/pgctree.html>.

Speaking of Christmas, is it better to write a letter to Santa on a full stomach or an empty stomach?

(It's better to write it on paper!)

After the excitement, Pammie Pigeon returned to the city. She went to sleep at 8 p.m. and slept 10 hours. What time did she wake up?

THE ARTS

Learning to draw is easy if you start with simple shapes. A cat is lots of circles. Draw one fat circle for the face. Draw a fatter circle for the body, little half-circles for paws, and tiny circles for eyes. Add triangles for ears and some straight lines for whiskers. You have a cat!

A rabbit is even easier. Draw a large circle for the body. Draw a small circle on top for the head and a tiny circle inside the large circle near the bottom for a fluffy tail. Draw two tall triangles for the ears. You drew a rabbit!

THE BEST I CAN BE

Peggy Porcupine was nervous because she had just left her mama's nest. She was so nervous she could not think straight and made a bad decision to gnaw at the bark on the prettiest tree in Farmer John's yard.

What are things that make you nervous or scare you? Do you have butterflies in your stomach when you give a report to your class? Are you worried because you do not understand how to do your homework? Do you think your friends will be mad at you because you made 100 on your math test? Take Pammie's advice: calm down, breathe deeply, stay calm, and think clearly, so you can use your problem-solving skills to decide what will be best to do.